THE SNAGGLE GROLLOP

DANIEL POSTGATE

ILLUSTRATED BY

NICK PRICE

Chicken House

'Can I have a **dog?**' asked Sam.
'**No,**' said his dad, 'I'll have to take
it for **walks** all the time.'

'Can I have a **cat?**' asked Sam.
'**No,**' said his mum, 'they leave
hair all over the place.'

This book belongs to

. . . .

. . . .

. . . .

For Alfie Bloom – DP
For Tilly – NP

© 2009 The Chicken House

First published in the United Kingdom in 2009 by
The Chicken House, 2 Palmer Street, Frome, Somerset, BA11 1DS
www.doublecluck.com

Text © 2009 Daniel Postgate
Illustrations © 2009 Nick Price

Designed by Ian Butterworth

Printed and bound in Singapore

1 3 5 7 9 10 8 6 4 2

British Library Cataloguing in Publication Data available
Library of Congress Cataloguing in Publication data available

HB ISBN: 978-1-904442-66-0
PB ISBN: 978-1-906427-00-9

'How about a **snagglegrollop**, can I have one of **them?**' asked Sam.

'What's a **snagglegrollop?**' asked Mum.
'I don't know,' said Sam,
'I just made it up.'

His parents laughed.
'Well ... if you just made it up,
then yes, you can have a
snagglegrollop!' said Dad.

After school Sam came home with a strange-looking creature.
'What on earth is that?' exclaimed Dad.

'It's a snagglegrollop,' said Sam.
'You said I could have one, remember?'

'Yes, but … no, but … but – oh heck,' spluttered Dad. 'Well, it's your responsibility. You are the one who has to look after it.'

The **snagglegrollop** took quite a lot of looking after.

It was very **hairy**, so it took a long time to **wash** . . .

. . . and dry.

It was very **big**,
so it needed **huge**
amounts of food.

And it had lots of **teeth**,
so it used an awful lot of **toothpaste**.

But it told **hilarious** jokes, and was a superb dancer,

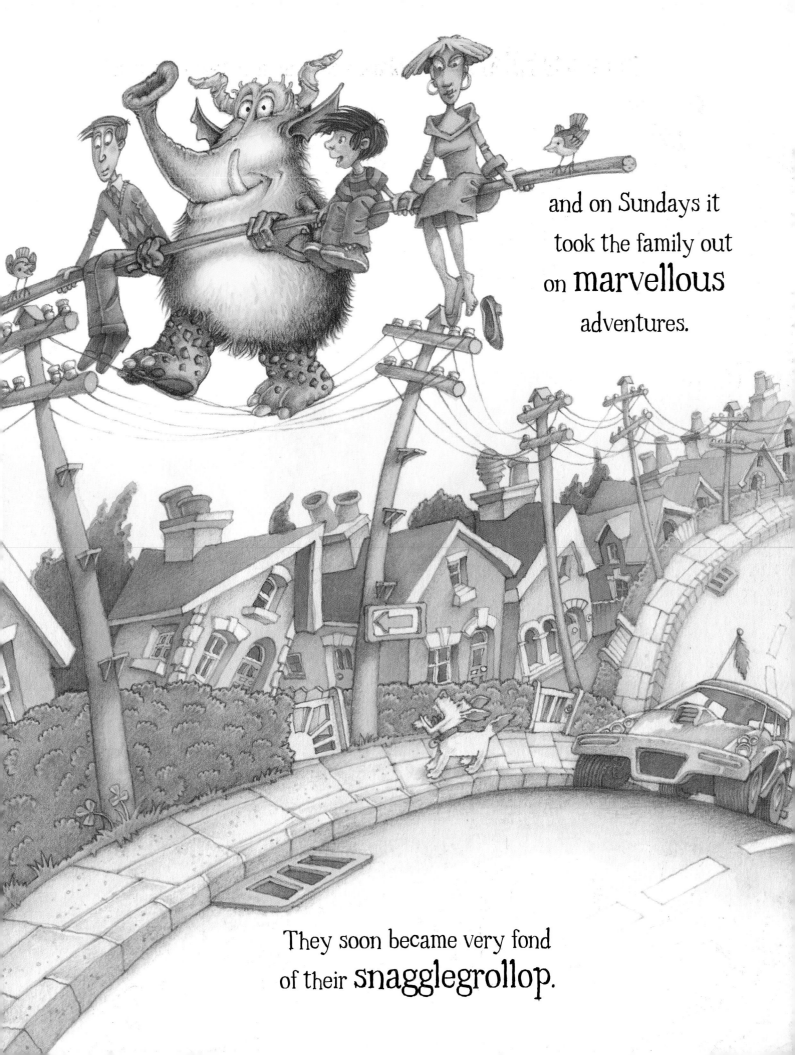

and on Sundays it took the family out on **marvellous** adventures.

They soon became very fond of their **snagglegrollop**.

But sometimes the **snagglegrollop**
seemed rather sad. At night it would sit
out on the roof of the garden shed and
stare at the stars.

One day at school, Emily Evans

(who Sam liked a lot but was too afraid to speak to)

said that her parents wouldn't let her have a cat.

'You could ask for a **snagglegrollop**,' said Sam, bravely.

'What's **that?**' asked Emily.

'I don't know,' said Sam, 'I made it up.'

Emily laughed. 'I think I would rather have a
quibblesnuff!' she said.

Sam, Dad and the **snagglegrollop** were playing hide-and-seek in the park one afternoon, when Emily arrived with her **quibblesnuff**.

Sam's snagglegrollop was **enchanted**.

They told each other **jokes** . . .

...and they **danced** together.

Then, hand in hand, they flew up into the sky

They flew once around the park, waved goodbye, and flew off into the distance.

'I didn't know they could do **that**,' said Sam. 'Do you think we'll ever see them again?'

'I don't know,' said Emily. 'I **suppose** it doesn't matter, as long as they're happy.'

'Can Emily come back to our house
after school one day?' Sam asked his dad.
'Of course she can,' said Dad.
'And can I have a dog?' asked Sam.
'Maybe,' said his dad, 'we'll see.'